Look and Find®

Disney · PIXAR

# Cars 3

195

95

pi kids®

**Phoenix International Publications, Inc.**

Chicago · London · New York · Hamburg · Mexico City · Paris · Sydney

**L**ightning McQueen is quicker than quick, faster than fast...he is speed! He lives to push himself to the next level using all he learned from his former crew chief Doc Hudson. But a new opponent, a sleek next-generation racer named Jackson Storm, proves that he's the fastest car on the track!

Can you speed through the scene and find these high-revving racers?

If Lightning is going to stay in the game, he needs a new training strategy. He needs to work out his wheels with the best of the best! When he arrives at the Rust-eze Racing Center, his new trainer Cruz Ramirez demonstrates her technique on the state-of-the-art racing simulator.

Tour the Rust-eze Racing Center for these precision training gadgets:

ENGINE R

Laps
261/500

MPH
193

**A**fter Lightning struggles through his training exercises and crashes into the simulator screen, his sponsor Sterling gives him one last shot: win the Florida 500...or retire from racing. Lightning and Cruz hit the beach to practice, but Cruz's high-tech training hasn't prepared her for sand!

Comb the beach for these objects:

oil cans

this gadget

this thingamajig

simulator training manual

flag

garbage can

On the way to the Florida 500, Lightning and Cruz wind up in the middle of the Thunder Hollow Crazy Eight demolition derby! Their competitors are a gang of battling beaters who love to get smash-happy. Lightning and Cruz need to drive—and think—fast if they want to hold on to their bumpers!

Can you find these crushed and careening car parts?

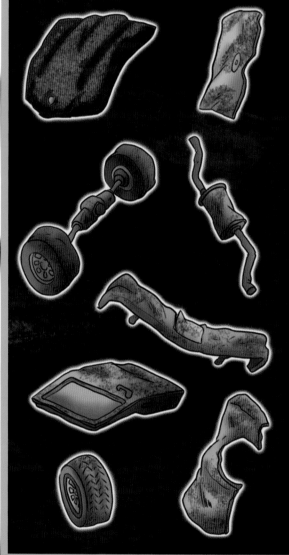

Welcome to... THUN HOLL

When Lightning and Cruz visit Doc Hudson's old racetrack, they meet racing legends River Scott, Junior Moon, and Louise Nash, and Doc's former crew chief Smokey. Smokey cuts right to the chase, telling Lightning he'll never be as fast as Storm. But he *can* be smarter.

Peruse the hallowed walls of the Cotter Pin and find these photos of Doc and other racing legends:

Lightning trains with Smokey like he's never trained before. He heightens his horsepower by driving with a trailer in tow and refines his reflexes by dodging tractors. Cruz acts as Lightning's sparring partner—and starts to reveal her own solid skills on the speedway!

Swerve through the training gauntlet and identify these tractors:

In the middle of the Florida 500, Lightning thinks as fast as he drives and decides that Cruz should finish the race. It's the perfect chance for him to help Cruz show the world she is a racer. Lightning takes over as crew chief, and Cruz takes the chance and revs with it. In a classic Doc Hudson maneuver, she flips over Storm to take the lead—and win!

Grab your binoculars and scan the stands for these friends and spectators:

Fillmore

Mater

Junior Moon

this fan

Louise Nash

Smokey

**C**ruz always had the engine of a champion—she just needed a chance to put it to the test! Cruz and Lightning team up to share the victory. Now, they'll use that team spirit as they look ahead to new challenges!

It's a heckuva win! Turn on your headlights and find these racing items:

blown tire

banner

flag

trophy

oil can

racing guide

**Put it in reverse all the way to the race scene and find these signs and banners:**

**Racers, start your simulators! Zoom back to the Rust-eze Racing Center and find these flags on the simulator screens:**

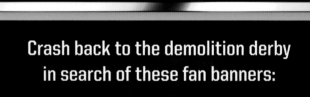

**Take a long drive back to the beach and find these briny items:**

this driftwood

this rock

sign

life preserver

this sea grass

this fence

**Crash back to the demolition derby in search of these fan banners:**

**Tastes great! Less viscosity! Pull up a bucket seat at the Cotter Pin and find these beverages:**

**Veer back to the tractor-filled training course and play your own game of dodge-bale as you spot these hay bundles:**

**Accelerate back to the Florida 500 and spot these numbers:**

**Flash back to the Florida 500 victory scene and zoom in on these cameras:**

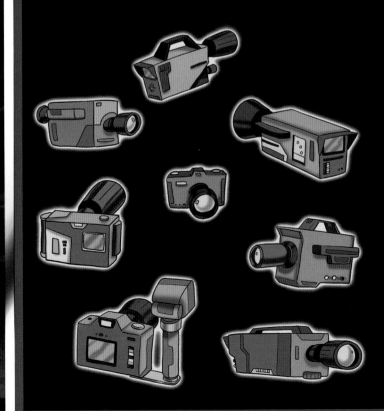